DO YOU ENJOY BEING FRIGHTENED?

WOULD YOU RATHER HAVE
NIGHTMARES
INSTEAD OF SWEET DREAMS?

ARE YOU HAPPY ONLY WHEN
SHAKING WITH FEAR?

CONGRATULATIONS ! ! ! !

YOU'VE MADE A WISE CHOICE.

THIS BOOK IS THE DOORWAY
TO ALL THAT MAY FRIGHTEN YOU.

GET READY FOR

COLD, CLAMMY SHIVERS
RUNNING UP AND DOWN YOUR SPINE!

NOW, OPEN THE DOOR–
IF YOU DARE ! ! ! !

Shivers

GUESS WHO'S COMING FOR DINNER?

M. D. Spenser

Plantation, Florida

Published by Paradise Press, Inc. by arrangement with River Publishing, Inc. All
right, title and interest to the "SHIVERS" logo and design are owned by River
Publishing, Inc. No portion of the "SHIVERS" logo and design may be reproduced
in part or whole without prior written permission from River Publishing, Inc. An
application for a registered trademark of the "SHIVERS" logo and design is pend-
ing with the Federal Patent and Trademark office.

ISBN 1-57657-055X

EXCLUSIVE DISTRIBUTION BY PARADISE PRESS, INC.

Cover Design by George Paturzo
Cover Illustration by Eddie Roseboom

Printed in the U.S.A.
30585

To Allen, who likes a good story

GUESS WHO'S COMING FOR DINNER?

Chapter One

Looking back, Josh thought Michael Sturdevant had always seemed a bit on the odd side, but Josh had always chalked that up to Michael's personality.

Michael was quiet and withdrawn. He was also gawky and gangly-limbed and awkward.

All those traits were the opposite of Josh Jenings. Josh was the school soccer star. He was outgoing, and he always had buddies around before and after school, and in the lunchroom saving a space for him at their table.

Michael, on the other hand, seemed to have no friends at Thomas Jefferson Middle. Well, yes, he'd had several over the years, Josh seemed to recall — other oddball kids in need of oddball friends.

But they always disappeared, somehow. They quit coming to school, perhaps because they transferred — or perhaps, as some kids joked, because Michael's blah personality just scared them away.

But Josh would learn that it was not Michael who scared the temporary friends away. Nor could it be said they went away of their own accord.

They just went to the Sturdevants' for dinner and never came back.

*   *   *

Of course, Josh had none of this in mind when he noticed Michael sitting by himself one day, in the far corner of the lunchroom.

There was no tray on Michael's table.

Like all the kids at Thomas J., Michael was required to go to the cafeteria at lunch hour. But Josh, who was usually surrounded by a swarm of other twelve-year-olds, had never paid attention to whether Michael ever actually ate.

The day he noticed the thin, dark boy hunched over a chessboard in the corner, eyeing his chessmen the way other kids eyed their chicken sandwiches, Josh was floored.

Michael was playing chess, sitting on one side of a chessboard filled with black and ivory chessmen. Every now and then, very deliberately, he moved a piece.

"Hey there, man," Josh called. "Are you playing chess by yourself?"

Michael, who was used to teasing, must have thought Josh was about to launch into a full-scale taunting session. He kept his head lowered and only half-raised his dark eyes.

"Yeah, so what?" he answered.

"Well," Josh said, stepping closer, "I like chess too. Does it help any to practice alone?"

He was not teasing. Because, though Josh had a lot of friends, he could rarely find anyone who liked to play chess.

Both his parents were serious career people. They never had time for a drawn-out game like chess.

And his little sister Megan — well, forget that! Even if she weren't despicable in general, she would never be interested in an intelligent game like chess. Although she claimed to be highly intelligent. Constantly.

Josh was going to ask for a chess instruction CD ROM for his birthday, but that was a ways off. He had mastered all sorts of chess openings he had studied in a dime store book. But a good middle game was far more important.

He needed someone to practice his tactics with.

"Sure, you can practice alone," Michael said, looking up with a flicker of interest. "I'm really just making notations. Of course, it's best to have a part-

ner, but this is good practice. My little sister Gladys —
well, she can play, but she really goes for the jugular,
you know. But," he added with a sheepish smile,
"when I play her, I get eaten alive. It gets old."

Josh had never heard Michael say this much in
all the years they had been in the same class. Maybe it
was because he had never paid attention.

Michael did seem to have a sense of humor.
And he knew exactly what he was talking about where
chess was concerned. Josh was intrigued.

"Hoo, boy," he said with a grin. "Do I know
about the annoying little sister bit! But mine isn't even
that evolved. I guess yours at least comes in handy for
chess practice."

Michael kept his eyes on his trial game, but
some clouds seemed to pass over his face.

"Let's just say I wish Gladys wasn't quite as
blood-thirsty as she is," he said.

Chapter Two

"Hey, Jennings, old buddy! Where've you been lately?"

Chet Carter stalked up to Josh's locker. Danny Sims followed close on his heels.

Both boys wore white soccer sweaters with the maroon TJ letters, and white T-shirts and blue jeans.

It was their uniform. Josh wore exactly the same thing.

"Well," Josh said slowly, shutting his locker with his elbow, "I've just been doing some other stuff."

This was the second crummy locker he'd gotten in a row. At least this one closed — after a good pounding.

Last year, he'd had to tie his locker with twine to keep it closed. Fortunately, Josh didn't care if every textbook he had was stolen.

His real treasures were in his gym locker: his cleats and his Thomas Jefferson jersey, with its win-

5

ning number 12, a number he'd held onto for three years.

"Yeah, like what?" Chet asked, leaning on the adjacent locker. He watched with amusement as Josh struggled with his locker door.

Finally, Josh managed to slam the door shut. He shackled it with his combination lock. He turned to Chet and Danny with a sarcastic smile.

"Since when did I have to fax you guys my schedule every day?" he said. He grabbed Chet's arm and playfully pushed him against the locker. "Maybe it's about time to get interested in things other than soccer, for a change."

"Maybe it's time to be worrying about geometry," Chet said. "Wicked Warner is popping a lot of tests these days. And the only person good at geometry is that Michael What's-his-name. What a weird dude."

"It's Michael Sturdevant," Josh said.

The eyebrows of the other two boys shot up. Josh felt as if he'd been caught doing something wrong.

What was wrong with hanging out with somebody new for a change, Josh thought. Sure, Michael seemed strange at first — anyone that deliberate and calculating would. Josh figured that anyone who'd had so many friends take a hike on him would naturally be that way.

He wasn't actually friends with Michael, either. He just admired the guy's chess game. They had played at lunch several times, and twice before school.

It was frustrating, too. By the end of all the games they'd played so far, all Josh's men — he'd always be white, Michael black — would be yanked from the board and stored in the little cedar chest Michael carried around with him. Josh got slaughtered in every game.

It bothered Josh a little that, during their cafeteria games, he always had to break for lunch, because he was starving. He'd be distracted while Michael, whom Josh had never seen eat anything, could study the board the entire time.

Josh suspected that gave Michael a definite edge. But what could he do about it?

Michael turned down all the half-hamburgers and half-macaroni and cheeses Josh offered him.

Josh couldn't make Michael eat, but perhaps he could distract him with a question.

"Hey Michael," he asked one day, as Michael was about to clean up on the chessboard again, "do you ever hang out with anyone else?"

Michael paled, and seemed to withdraw into himself. Suddenly, Josh saw the shy, awkward boy everybody else saw.

Oh, man, I insulted him! thought Josh.

He was actually beginning to like Michael. When he played chess and joked, he "got a personality," Josh told Chet and Danny.

"Ah," Michael answered slowly, "I can't really answer that."

Josh turned back to the chessboard.

Aha, it had worked! Michael had missed a move! His black king had a means of escape, but old Mike had failed to take it.

Josh smiled sympathetically.

"Checkmate," he said.

Boy, did that feel good after all those weeks of getting trounced.

"Sorry, Michael my man, I know if you'd had your head together just now you'd never have made it so easy."

Michael faked wide-eyed astonishment. Then he shrugged.

"You ought to play Gladys sometime," he said. "She never loses *her* head."

Chapter Three

Josh didn't try any more diversionary tactics again.

He had wondered if it was cheating, and he was not a cheater — plus, he was beginning to appreciate Michael more and more. Not only for the help Michael gave him with chess. He was helping Josh with geometry too.

"Think of it like a chessboard," Michael advised, "how each piece can only move in certain ways, and you have to follow the rules to score the result you want. But you can get creative with your moves. And in geometry, it's the same, except with shapes and theorems. The steps in a hypothesis have to follow one another exactly in order to get the right answer, but you can use your imagination."

It really worked to think of it that way! Josh had always been uncomfortable with math and tests, but he felt more confident when he imagined himself sitting at a chessboard that happened to offer up geometry problems.

Wicked Warner, the math teacher, had even smiled at Josh after she'd handed back the pop geometry quizzes last Tuesday.

This was certainly new — she hardly ever graced the jocks with so much as a pleasant look. Josh had noticed that Wicked Warner always had a smile for Michael, though. Now he understood why.

That night before dinner, Josh decided to do something a little different. Instead of talking to his parents about soccer, or something idiotic Chet had done at school today, he reached into his backpack.

"A piece of schoolwork? This, from Joshua?" his father said in mock surprise.

"Josh brought home schoolwork?" his mother asked, looking up from the briefcase she'd just popped open on her knees.

As Mr. Jennings scanned the paper, his normally grave expression melted into a smile.

"Josh, an A-minus in geometry. I'm quite proud."

He reached over and grasped Josh's shoulder in a half-hug.

"Oh, Josh!" his mother cried. "An A-minus? Is it true, Ben?"

Josh blushed a deep purple. Why didn't he get this embarrassed when he scored the winning goal in a soccer game?

"It was a pop test too," he found himself piping up. Like some math geek! He could have kicked himself for saying that. But he *was* proud.

Megan, his little sister, had been showing off the contents of her school bag since kindergarten. She had obviously been preparing to brag about her grades from today, too, like she always did. Because she seemed disappointed now.

"Josh has been hanging out with the strangest guy, Mom and Dad," she said. "I mean, this guy's sister is eight years old, a year younger than me — "

"Than I," Mrs. Jennings corrected.

"Than I," Megan continued, "and she is so weird. Her name's Gladys. Isn't that weird too? Anyway, she's so strange even some of the older kids are afraid of her."

Chapter Four

Mr. Jennings scowled at Megan.

Mrs. Jennings, who now held the golden geometry quiz, joined him in a curt frown.

"Megan Jennings, who Josh's friends are is his business, just like your friends are your business," she said. "Josh and Heidi haven't gotten along a day in their lives, and that will never affect your right to have her over."

Heidi was Megan's best friend. Josh couldn't stand her. She was nine, the same age as Megan. But she was five times as bad as Megan at her worst. Heidi always one-upped you or challenged whatever you said.

Josh could never think up a comeback to her smart-aleck comments until it was way too late.

"Well," Megan sniffed, "I got an A, not an A minus, in spelling. Does anybody care?"

She clamped her straight hair with the colorful cloth-covered barrette she always wore, the one Mrs. Jennings had brought her from Mexico.

"Yes, we care," Mr. Jennings said, "but may we please compliment Josh on something — er, unusual and great, that he's done?"

Megan gave a loud sigh and thrust her hands dramatically in the air.

"What does this mean? Like, do I have to join the swim team and win a medal now, or something?"

Everybody ignored her as they got the plates and silverware out for supper.

Mr. Jennings got some frozen meals out of the freezer and lined them up in front of the microwave so people could pick. On workdays, instant meals were the usual Jennings family fare.

Megan scowled over her steaming Australian pot pie.

"Have you ever seen Michael eat anything?" she asked, raising a forkful of peas and carrots. "Don't you think that's weird?"

"Not really," Josh lied.

Of course, not eating at mealtimes was weird. But the only mealtime he spent with Michael was lunch. For all he knew, the guy ate breakfast and dinner — heck, maybe even a midnight snack.

13

"Would it *shock* you," Megan went on, waving her uneaten forkful around in an artistic motion, "to know what Gladys Sturdevant *really* brings for lunch?"

Chapter Five

"*No*," Josh answered. "What do I care what she brings for lunch?"

A lump began to form in the back of his throat.

Megan looked uneasy. Her fork fell to her plate with a clank.

"I'm not sure," she said. "I was hoping you might know."

"OK, that's enough," Mr. Jennings broke in. "I don't care what somebody else eats for lunch, I just want to eat *my* dinner."

He smiled at his chicken dumplings with mashed potatoes and cast Mrs. Jennings an appreciative look.

"This looks good, hon," he said.

Mrs. Jennings beamed.

"Why thank you, darling," she said. "It just leapt off the grocery store shelf at me. It had your name written all over it."

Mr. Jennings nodded at Josh.

"I don't care if your new friend's weird or not, son," he said. "I think he's a good influence."

"Michael doesn't have any other friends," Megan said. "Neither does Gladys. She had one last year, I think. Bessie Butler went home with her after school a couple of times. But then Bessie just vanished."

Mrs. Jennings raised her head sharply from her plate of El Presidento cheese enchiladas. She was a lawyer, so people's problems always interested her.

"Megan, I'm sure Bessie just changed schools," she said. "One of her parents must have been transferred to another city."

Megan shook her head.

"Nobody said anything about her transferring, and they usually do," she said. "I know, because I listened for it when I stopped seeing her on the bus."

"Nosy," Josh said.

"They always announce it over the intercom," Megan went on. "Like when Maurice had to move to New York, they announced it. But we knew months before that. Maurice told everybody he was 'blowing this Popsicle stand.' "

Mr. Jennings adjusted his rather large body in his chair.

"That's quite a cliché," he said. He owned a company that published newsletters.

"Megan, a person can move away without officially announcing it to everybody," Josh said. "They can just go fill out some papers in the principal's office."

He scooped up great forkfuls of steak, gravy and au gratin potatoes. Frozen dinners had come a long way.

Of course, they hadn't always eaten them so often. Mr. Jennings used to publish newsletters from home, and he would prepare the family meals. But since his company moved out of the spare bedroom into offices on Ward Street, he no longer had time.

Josh was starving. As his chess game had improved, his sessions with Michael had extended to the half-hour after school during which kids waited for the bus. That cut out Josh's afternoon snack.

But, even as he gulped his food, Megan's prattling about kids disappearing bothered him.

What was the deal? Gladys's friends disappeared, too? So it wasn't only Michael's friends that beat it. Did they both have the same scary personality?

It didn't make sense. Josh had discovered that Michael's personality wasn't scary at all. He didn't even seem withdrawn any more. He was funny and interesting and smart.

Clearing the last pea off his plate, he tried to shrug off his worries. It probably wasn't even true that all of Michael's friends disappeared. Nobody paid attention to Michael. How could they know who his friends were?

Although Josh did remember when Billy Johns went away. There had been no announcement then, either. Usually when someone left school, everybody knew the reason. Sometimes, people even held a good-bye party with cupcakes and colas.

Though it was over a year ago, Josh remembered that there had been no party for Billy Johns.

Billy just stopped coming to school. Nobody ever said where he'd gone.

Chapter Six

The discussion about missing friends bothered Josh for the next few days. Still, he looked forward to his next chess game with Michael.

He had even beaten Michael once.

Sure, Michael had been preoccupied that day — very preoccupied — over something he didn't want to discuss. Josh didn't push or ask too many questions. He remembered how Michael had reacted to the question about whether he had any other friends.

It was fun having a chess partner. Learning the game, and understanding its principles, made Josh feel smart. Possibly for the first time in his life.

He'd felt special before. He excelled in sports. He had lots of friends. Girls considered him good-looking.

But with chess came a feeling of braininess that made Josh feel as happy as he felt winning a soccer tournament. He, Josh Jennings, could — every now and then — win a battle of wits!

19

His old daydreams had centered around soccer, perhaps scoring the winning goal. Now he had a new fantasy: Heidi would admit that she'd always thought Josh was brilliant, and that she'd acted like a ninny because she was jealous. All she had ever really wanted in this world was to learn chess from the great grand master, Joshua Jennings, who could wallop even the most intelligent computer in the world. . . .

Michael murmured to himself, shattering Josh's daydream. They were sitting in the lunchroom studying the chessboard.

Michael ate nothing, as usual. Josh nibbled on a bag lunch he'd brought to avoid the distraction of standing in the cafeteria line.

"You just let me capture your pawn *en passant*," Michael said. "See, it keeps you from taking advantage of the two-square first-move rule."

He whipped Josh's white pawn off the board and placed his black pawn in the square just behind where the white one had stood.

"OK." Josh chomped on his bologna and cheese sandwich. He didn't mind Michael giving him a pointer or two. He could use them against Michael later.

"Boo!" a voice shouted in Josh's ear.

Josh jumped. Several of the white chess pieces rattled to the linoleum floor.

20

Chapter Seven

Chet Carter leered at Josh.

"Jennings, my man," he said, "you are truly turning into a patsy now. You're jumping like a kid afraid of a mouse."

Chet grabbed an orange chair and pulled it backwards to their table.

"All right, I give up," he said, folding his arms across the back of the chair. "What is so great about this egghead game? You sure spend a lot of time at it."

Danny Sims, naturally, was tagging along with Chet. He, too, dragged up a chair.

Chet stared into Josh's face, trying to get on his nerves. So did Danny.

It worked.

"Guys, you know Michael, right?" Josh asked, trying to sound casual. His question came out in a croak. He wasn't comfortable having to balance his usual set of friends with Michael.

"Charmed, I'm sure," said Chet, grabbing his cap off his head in a grandiose gesture.

"Hi," said Danny, reaching for his cap, too, but stopping when he realized he wasn't wearing one. He blushed and put his hand back in his lap.

Josh looked at him incredulously. Would this guy ever get a mind of his own, or would he always just do whatever Chet did?

"Hello," Michael said coolly. "This is a serious game. That's why we're over here in the corner. Please be quiet if you're going to hang around."

Chet and Danny stared.

So did Josh, surprised that Michael had such nerve. Chet could be a bully sometimes.

Josh was impressed that Michael had stood up for himself. In the past, he had never reacted when someone teased him. But now Chet and Danny apparently threatened to interfere with an activity he found important.

"Oh, well excuse me," Chet said. "And all this time I thought you were over in the corner because you don't do lunch and you're always alone. Gee, stupid me."

He scowled and reached for the chessboard.

Michael shifted the board several inches away from Chet. Josh was stunned at his boldness.

"Sorry," Chet said.

Chet glared at him. But Michael shot him a smile.

"No problem," he said. "Now, watch this, I'm going to do a neat move here, one that our man Josh has made possible by his infinite kindness. I'm going to search and destroy. First, Josh, you agree the pieces that got bumped off during that interruption are back in proper position?"

Reluctantly, Josh agreed, knowing full well something bad was about to happen to his lucky white chessmen.

Suddenly, a shriek interrupted them.

"Mi-*chael*!"

All four heads swiveled to see who had made such a shrill and unpleasant noise.

They saw, striding across the lunchroom toward them, a pudgy girl with dark pigtails, beady eyes, and the sourest expression Josh had ever seen on a human being.

Her fat little arms pumped with each step. Her whiny, insistent voice grated like fingernails on a blackboard.

"Mi-*chael*!" she screeched. "I've got a bone to pick with you!"

Chapter Eight

"Uh, you guys," Michael mumbled. "This is my sister Gladys."

Gladys shifted back and forth. *Scrape, scrape.*

Josh's eyes flew to her feet. She wore a pair of clunky hobnailed boots.

His eyes flickered back to her face. He could have sworn he saw her lick her lips when she glanced at him. Then she stamped her foot — *clink!* — on the worn linoleum.

He was too busy marveling at the sheer creepiness of Gladys to give the lip-licking much thought. She was just a plump little girl, younger than all of them, even Megan. She even wore pigtails.

But, somehow, the hairdo made her look even scarier. Because under it was a mature-looking face. Like Michael's, but more cunning.

And the boots! They were like dog-kicking boots, or boots some jail warden might wear to keep her inmates in line.

Above the boots was a pair of fat shins bruised blue and yellow, and scabby knees. On her stocky body hung a drab blue dress with faded yellow polka dots.

The dress matched the bruises on her shins.

Something about Gladys intimidated Josh. Something beyond her appearance.

Again Gladys pierced the uncomfortable silence.

"Did you eat a cupcake in class this morning?" she shrieked into Michael face. She spat out the word "cupcake."

"N-no," Michael stammered.

Gladys cast her beady eyes at Josh.

"You in his class?" she asked. "Did he eat one?"

Her eyes were black, and sharp as tacks. She looked Josh up and down. This time there was no mistaking it: she licked her lips with a flicker of pink tongue.

As Josh opened his mouth to reply, he saw Michael slowly shake his head no.

"No," He tried to control his shaking bottom lip. His palms filled with sweat.

Gladys whirled back to Michael.

"I saw that!" she said. "And I see icing on your chin!"

Chet jumped up so fast that his chair clattered over. Danny had already raced for the lunchroom door.

"Uh, thanks for the chess lesson, dudes," Chet said. He crossed his eyes at the back of Gladys's head and tipped his cap to Josh. "Soccer after school, Jennings, my man?"

"You ate a cupcake!" Gladys screamed at Michael. She said "cupcake" the way someone else would say "cockroach."

"Who gave it to you?" she demanded. "I'm gonna tell."

Suddenly, she stormed out the door, her hobnails clacking on the floor.

Michael was twelve shades paler than usual, if that was possible. Josh had seen the terror in Michael's eyes when he shook his head, signaling Josh to tell Gladys "no." What would have happened if Josh hadn't seen the cue, and had said "yes"?

What the dickens was so awful about eating a cupcake? Wicked Warner had brought them in because she had promised she would if everyone made a C or above on the geometry test.

And they all had — including Josh, who had come back from the math-impaired with another A-minus.

Then Josh realized that the cupcake was the first thing he'd ever seen Michael eat, and he had almost swallowed it whole.

Were the Sturdevants violently against sweets or something?

And Josh had seen the way Michael stood up to Chet. Why had he cowered before his little sister?

He decided the pudgy little thing must be even more threatening than she looked.

Chapter Nine

"I think my mom's ordering pizza tonight," Josh said. "Why don't you come by, have a few slices?"

Michael accepted eagerly. About half an hour later, they were both seated in the Jennings' living room.

"What kind of pizza do you think your mom will order?" Michael asked eagerly, rearranging his gawky legs on Mrs. Jennings' beige flowered ottoman.

"Hmm — veggie, probably," Josh said, flipping through the TV guide for a good sports show. "Green peppers, mushrooms, onions and stuff. We eat a lot of quickie meals around here but Mom tries to be healthy."

He grabbed the TV remote off the coffee table and switched to the tennis finals. It was better than nothing.

Then, remembering Michael was his guest, Josh added, "If that doesn't sound cool, maybe

Mom'll let us crumble some bacon or something on top."

"Oh, no!" Michael answered quickly. "No, I like veggies."

He seemed so happy about a pizza!

Josh loved to eat, but Michael hung on every ingredient. They were talking about pizza, not homemade lasagna or Belgian waffles, for heaven's sake.

"Can you name the veggies that might be on it again?" Michael asked.

Josh looked at him strangely.

"Just kidding," Michael said, and forced a little laugh. "I just don't get fresh vegetables very often. I guess you could say my family is the reverse of yours."

"So that was what that cupcake thing was about?" Josh asked. "Your family has a rule against sweets?"

Michael managed a grim smile.

"Not exactly," he said.

Josh pondered Michael's strange eating habits. He ate the cupcake, and he was most definitely up for this pizza. He did not eat in the cafeteria. His sister hung out in the cafeteria at the same time.

That was it: He ate only when his sister was not around.

He sneaked his food. And when he got the opportunity to eat, he relished it.

Michael blushed and stared at the floor. He met Josh's eyes, then looked away bashfully.

"OK," he said, finally. "I have been dreading this moment, but I guess we can't go on being friends any longer without you knowing some important things. I've got to be able to trust you."

Josh nodded uncertainly.

He was in the safety of his own home. His mother would show up any minute.

Still, something was wrong. And weird.

"Look, I know you and Chet are friends," Michael went on, "but somebody like Chet can't know what I'm about to tell you. Understand?"

"Yeah," Josh said. And he did.

He and Chet had hung out together since kindergarten. Chet even shared his hatred of Heidi. But Chet was also a blabbermouth. And he had not been nice to Michael.

"OK," Michael said, drawing a deep breath. "You've met Gladys, and you know me. We're — we don't, um, do things the usual way. Like, you and your family don't eat traditional meals, exactly? Um, neither do we."

A chill crept across Josh's shoulders. But he tried to be pleasant.

"Yeah," he said. "Around here, it's like, would you like your dinner frozen, frozen or frozen?"

Michael shook his head.

"I don't have the luxury of choice, I'm afraid," he said. "So mostly I choose not to eat at all."

Josh's body felt as frozen as the Swiss steak he'd had last night.

The back door burst open. He jumped.

"Yoo-hoo!" called Mrs. Jennings from the kitchen. "Dinner's on, but I need somebody to take these pizza boxes before I drop them."

Relief flooded into Michael's face. Josh knew he would not hear the rest of the story — not tonight anyway. His mother would keep Michael talking. She would interview him like she was grilling a prospective client. He and Michael would never be alone.

Somehow, even though Michael was his buddy and all, Josh was glad.

Chapter Ten

"All right everybody, what's your pick?" Mrs. Jennings sang out. "Veggie or extra-lean Canadian bacon?"

She handed two pizza boxes to Josh, who moved them to the kitchen counter and propped back the cardboard lids.

"Canadian bacon can be extra-lean?" Megan asked, sliding into the kitchen in her socks.

Her ponytail was wrenched sideways. She must have been lying on the bed talking on the phone. Probably talking to Hideous Heidi.

"Oh, you're Michael Sturdevant," she said.

She toyed with her ponytail, readjusted her Mexico barrette and stared at Michael. Then — rather nervously, Josh thought — she reached for a plate.

"Oh, you're Michael!" Mrs. Jennings said, turning around.

"Yes ma'am," Michael said. His eyes were fastened on the pizza Megan was pulling from one of the boxes. "Veggie for me, definitely, please."

Josh, Megan and their mother watched Michael curiously. He was so anxious. So . . . *hungry*.

"Mom, this is Michael Sturdevant," Josh said.

Michael dived into the pizza box and happily heaped four slices of veggie pizza onto his plate.

"Help yourself," Mrs. Jennings told him. She was sizing him up, Josh could tell.

"So, Mr. Sturdevant," she continued. "You are the great geometry guru."

The great *hungry* geometry guru, Josh thought. He watched with amazement as Michael laid his pizza slices on top of each other, then rolled the whole pile into a hefty pizza sausage.

"Josh is pretty good at geometry in his own right," Michael said. "He's a good chess player. Good chess players make good mathematicians."

"Good thing the rest of us like Canadian bacon," Megan said, and she didn't even sound sarcastic. "Hey," she said, turning to Josh, "I heard Mrs. Warner gave you guys cupcakes this morning. Why'd she do that?"

Michael suddenly looked as if he were about to choke.

"Because she wanted to," Josh retorted.

33

Mrs. Jennings wore the concerned look she assumed in PTA meetings when she spoke about underprivileged kids.

"Dear," she said to Michael, "I want you to just help yourself to all the pizza you want, and for you to come over any time. There's always a hot meal for you here."

"Though it was probably frozen first," Josh added.

Josh could tell his mother was charmed off her feet by Michael.

"Yes," she said gently. "Let's work on putting some meat on those bones."

Chapter Eleven

The next day Wicked Warner began her class by waving the red geometry book at them and then dropping it in one of her desk drawers.

"OK everyone," she said. "Our geometry unit is over for now."

There was a low whistle, followed by a hearty round of applause.

"Yippee!" a voice called from the back.

"We'll be working on *algebra* for the next two months," Wicked Warner said.

Groans took over. Josh's stomach dropped. How would he ever survive algebra?

"But first I want to make mention of a student in this class who has markedly improved in geometry," Wicked Warner went on. "The most improved is Joshua Jennings. You have made remarkable progress in geometry, young man. Playing sports doesn't mean you have to be a mediocre student."

Wicked Warner gestured for Josh to stand. He did so reluctantly.

"I'm going to telephone your parents to tell them how pleased I've been lately with your work," she said.

"I'm going to phone your parents," Chet whispered behind Josh. "You're just won-duh-ful, dear boy."

Josh's face reddened. But Chet was not going to ruin this moment for him. He was happy about it. He was proud, dang it.

"You may sit now, Joshua," Wicked Warner said, and the class tittered as Josh realized he was still standing. He sank back into his seat, flushing scarlet.

Class dragged. Josh didn't understand the preliminary algebra problems.

"Everybody!" Wicked Warner yelled as everyone started spilling out of the room after the bell. "Hang on to the homework you were going to hand in today, perfect it and give it to me tomorrow. Since I'm dining out, I won't have time to correct your papers."

She seemed very happy about this dinner. Maybe she didn't get out much.

"But you'd better remember your papers tomorrow," she called. "Or heads will roll."

*　　*　　*

At the lunch table, Michael sat with his head in his hands, looking as if a weight lay on his thin bony back. He hadn't set up the chessboard yet.

"Aren't we playing, man?" Josh asked.

Michael cleared his throat and combed the room with his dark eyes, as if hoping for an interruption. There was none.

"Help me keep Wicked Warner away from my house tonight," he said.

"What can I do about it?" Josh asked.

"Maybe try to convince her you need help in algebra — say, with that homework she put off till tomorrow. Say you tried last night and couldn't do it. You want to keep your status as a most improved student. And you need help tonight."

"I have our first soccer practice today after school," Josh protested. "I can't miss it."

"I think I'm going to have to explain why all this is so important," Michael said with a sigh. "My family is going to — "

"Hey, wait, man," Josh stopped him. "It's OK, you don't — "

"Mi-*chael*!" screeched a voice, and without looking, Josh knew whose it was. "Guess who's coming for dinner!"

Chapter Twelve

"I know who's coming for dinner, Gladys," Michael said.

He just sat and looked at her. He seemed too tired to be afraid today.

"Ooo, goody. Is she here? Can you point her out to me?"

Gladys didn't even look at Josh today — to his relief. Still, the hair on the back of his neck stood up at the sight of her.

Michael shrugged and pointed to the teacher's table across the room. "Over there, Gladys. Tall, red hair, thin. Blue suit."

"Later!" Gladys shouted. She tore off, and for a frumpy kid in big boots, she moved incredibly fast. She was robust and energetic — the opposite of Michael.

"Maybe she'll give Mrs. Warner a warning, you know, scare her off," Michael explained to Josh. "She can't do anything in here."

Josh could see how Gladys could creep some-body out. He prayed Wicked Warner would indeed be scared off by her. That way he wouldn't have to help Michael keep her away.

"Uh, you said 'can't do anything in here.' What does that mean?" Josh asked.

"Never mind," Michael said. "Let's just focus on keeping her away. Do you have any other ideas to keep her from coming over?"

This would not have been Josh's choice of an after-school activity. But he felt responsible for Wicked Warner's safety. He sensed that she was in danger, and she had no clue.

"Well," Josh began, "what if Wicked, I mean Mrs. Warner came to *my* house? With you and your folks too? And even Gladys."

Michael shook his head.

"Me and Mrs. Warner, fine," he said. "Gladys and my parents, no. That's not safe."

"You said Gladys couldn't do anything here or at the teacher's table."

"Yes," Michael said. "But Gladys and my parents at your house, *away from a public place,* is defi-nitely not safe."

Chapter Thirteen

As they walked down the hall to history class, Josh made up his mind. There was nothing else he could do. And he sensed that this was somehow very important.

"I'll cut soccer today," he said. "I'll hold up Wicked Warner. I don't know how, but I'll do it. I might need Chet and Danny, too."

"If you think Chet would cooperate," Michael said with a sigh. "I don't trust Chet. But Danny's a good guy."

"Hey, wait a minute," Josh started. But defending Chet was useless. He was obnoxious.

"It'll be fine," he said. "Chet loves nothing more than to trick a teacher. He doesn't have to know that, in this case, it's for her own good. It'll be better if it seems like pure mischievousness."

"Mischievousness?" Had Josh ever used that word before? Wow, he even *sounded* smarter when he was around Michael.

Michael grinned. "I get your drift, man," he said.

"Man?" And Michael sounded cooler when he was with Josh.

"So Chet doesn't need to know the whole story," Michael said. "And Danny will do whatever Chet does. It should work out fine."

*   *   *

After school, Josh walked to the soccer field. He scoured the field for Chet and Danny. He tried to think about what he had to do, not why he had to do it.

But he couldn't fight the truth. And the truth made him sick to his stomach.

He knew the Sturdevants considered Wicked Warner more than just a dinner guest.

Could she be — the dinner?

41

Chapter Fourteen

Chet did not want to skip soccer, even for the sake of mischievousness.

"I've been waiting two months for this!" he said. "I won't make first string if I miss a practice!"

"OK," Josh said. "So you're going to let Michael get an awesome review from Wicked Warner, and allow him to one-up the rest of us. That's disappointing coming from you, but I guess I'll have to accept it."

Chet frowned.

"I thought you and Sturdevant were big friends," he said.

"Not really," Josh said with a shrug. "I think he's weird. He's nice to play chess with, but now that I'm practically doing as well in geometry as he is, I don't appreciate his kissing up to Wicked Warner, you know?"

Chet looked at Josh suspiciously.

"All right," he said finally. "We'll skip soccer. Danny, are you in?"

Danny had been sitting beside Chet, lacing up his new cleats and not really listening.

"Yeah, I'm in." he said. "In for what?"

Josh wished Michael was there to help. But Michael had said he was under his mother's orders to get home right after school, so he could help get ready for Wicked Warner's visit.

He didn't like putting Michael down, but he'd had to in order to get Chet to cooperate. He needed his cooperation to save Wicked Warner from the clutches of the Sturdevants.

They put their plan into action.

To get out of soccer, Chet and Danny faked stomach pains. Josh did not have to pretend. His stomach was doing flips and tying itself into knots.

All three boys clutched their stomachs and looked as ill as they could, for the benefit of Coach Lennick.

They trudged across the soccer field. As soon as they were out of Coach Lennick's sight, they sprinted full-tilt toward the math and science building. They had to get there while Wicked Warner was still in her classroom.

Josh was not even sure the building would still be open.

"Please be unlocked, please be unlocked," he prayed as he ran.

They reached the double doors. Josh yanked on the door handles.

They were locked.

Josh was frantic. They were too late! Wicked Warner was gone, already on her way to meet whatever fate awaited her at the Sturdevants'.

But Chet said she might still be in the building.

"They always lock up at 3:30," he said. "But I bet with all the homework Wicked Warner gives, she's one of those teachers who stays late. Let's check her room from the outside."

Josh and Danny followed Chet around the side of the building. They peeked in through the window of the last room in the wing. Stupid "math-is-fun" posters lined the walls. This was Wicked Warner's room, all right.

A shadow moved inside. Dark and tall.

"She's in there!" Danny cried. "What do we do now?"

"Pipe down, for starters," Chet said.

Josh's back hurt from hunching over. He tried to ignore the pain.

"Maybe we should knock on the window to get her attention," he said. "Let's let Wicked Warner know we're out here and just say we needed to talk to her, and there was no other way because the doors were locked."

"Nothing else to do," Chet said.

They stood and peered into the pale blue room. Then they noticed a second shadow lurking against the back wall.

The extra shadow was much shorter and fatter than Wicked Warner's.

"Who's that?" Danny whispered.

"Not sure yet," Chet said. He rapped on the window pane.

At that moment the shorter shadow darted behind Wicked Warner's tall one, and raised something big and clunky-looking right over the back of Wicked Warner's head.

Wicked Warner suddenly bent down to pick up something.

Crash! The object struck the window. Glass shattered.

The boys dived into the bushes as the object sailed over their heads. Shards of glass tinkled to the ground.

Trembling, Josh grasped the windowsill and pulled himself up. Slowly he raised his eyes.

Wicked Warner stood there, looking back at him. Her face was pale. She held her chalkboard pointer, which must have been what she had stooped to pick up.

Thank heavens for that, Josh thought. Otherwise, that clunky-looking object, whatever it was, would have slammed right into the back of her head!

Chapter Fifteen

"All right, what's going on, gentlemen?" Wicked Warner asked. "You will have to pay for this window, I am sure you know."

What? Josh thought. She was blaming the broken window on them? She must not have seen the shoe fly past her! From *inside*!

He scoured the bushes, and spotted the object not two feet from Chet.

It was a boot. A hob-nailed boot.

He whirled and stared back into the math room. The shorter shadow had retreated to the back of the room again.

Wicked Warner shoved open the broken window. "I want all three of you to get in here and have a seat." She rapped her pointer on a front row desk.

The boys found themselves climbing through the open window. You didn't argue with Wicked Warner.

Josh suddenly noticed that Gladys Sturdevant was sitting in Wicked Warner's chair. Gladys smiled maliciously and eyed the teacher as she paced the room.

"What's going on?" Wicked Warner demanded again, ignoring Gladys.

"Soccer ball!" Chet cried. "Lost our soccer ball in the bushes."

"If that soccer ball just broke that glass, then where is it?" Wicked Warner asked. "I hardly think any of you boys are that proficient at kicking a ball. Let's see, if the soccer field is one quarter-mile away from the building, and Chester can kick a ball one-seventh of a mile . . ."

"Wicked — I mean Mrs. Warner," Josh stammered, "you need — we need — help!"

He kept his eyes glued on Gladys. She wasn't the sort of person you could turn your back on. That boot in the bushes was evidence of that.

Wicked Warner sat on the edge of her desk. She seemed calmer. The desperate plea had gotten her attention. But now she was in front of Gladys again.

"Mrs. Warner, could you move over a little this way?" Josh asked feebly.

"What?" Wicked Warner looked perplexed.

Danny had been sitting quietly the entire time. Now he spoke.

"Mrs. Warner, you can't go to dinner tonight," he said. "You have to help us with our homework. Or we'll all fail!"

Josh watched Gladys slip out of Wicked Warner's chair and waddle to the window. She reached through the jagged glass and casually picked up the boot she'd thrown.

The boot had been at least seven feet from the window. How in the world, Josh wondered, did she do that?

She carried the boot back to the chair, and sat, once again, squarely behind Wicked Warner.

She did not put the boot back on.

Chapter Sixteen

The stern look on Wicked Warner's face melted a little around the eyes.

But, as always, Chet had to top everyone else.

"It's terrible, Mrs. Warner," he said. "We want so much to excel in algebra. Oh, please help us."

Wicked Warner pressed her lips tightly together.

"Well boys, as you see, I have company," she said. "Miss Gladys Sturdevant will be escorting me to dinner at her lovely home. A bit unexpected, being escorted, actually — I had expected to drive my own car."

Wicked Warner turned to Gladys, who was grinning in that awful way she had.

"But a polite gesture," Wicked Warner concluded.

She didn't look completely sold on the polite bit. She looked confused — like Chet with an algebra problem in front of him.

"We better go," Josh said. He didn't want to risk making Wicked Warner too mad.

"Hey, what about you helping us?" Chet demanded.

Wicked Warner smiled wryly.

"I should think that, since you've managed for two years in my math classes on your own, you can wait another day."

Their ploy had been working, at least halfway, but Chet had wrecked it!

"Take a stab at the homework tonight," the teacher said. "I will be available to help you tomorrow."

Josh decided they would just have to follow Wicked Warner. That shouldn't be too hard, he thought. She and Gladys must be walking, since Gladys couldn't drive.

"But — " Josh began one last time. He was interrupted by a sharp rap on the classroom door.

Wicked Warner looked up.

"The building is locked," she said. "Who could this be?"

She opened the door cautiously. Josh sneaked a look at Gladys, who sat looking as smug as ever.

A short, stocky woman with dark hair walked briskly through the doorway. When she saw all the people in the room, she stopped short.

"Why, um, y-you're up and about," she said to Wicked Warner, "How nice. And how *thin*!" She didn't sound very happy about the thin part.

"And you have company," she added.

Wicked Warner just stood there clutching her pointer, staring at the newcomer.

The woman wore a dowdy green dress and a pair of black patent leather pumps with spiky heels — like the ones Mrs. Jennings wore to a cocktail party.

She looked like Gladys, but not quite as scary. Surely, she was . . .

"I'm Mrs. Sturdevant," the woman said.

She turned to Gladys, who looked strangely shy.

"Why Gladdy, what happened with your boots?"

Gladys scowled.

"She was too quick," she whined. "Plus these guys came up. It wasn't my fault!"

"Then I'm going to have to get your father. My, look at all these people here!"

She looked long and hard at Danny, and then at Chet. Finally, her eyes came to rest on Josh.

She looked him up and down thoroughly. It was a bone-chilling stare, worse than the once-over Gladys had given him when they first met in the lunchroom.

Mrs. Sturdevant's face broke into a grin.

"Oh," she said under her breath. "How adorable. A nice, big boy. I could just eat you up!"

Chapter Seventeen

Wicked Warner held the classroom door open for them as they filed out. Their footsteps echoed in the empty hall.

Josh would have loved nothing more than to bolt through the front door of the building and run to the soccer field, where all was safe.

Gladys kept stopping so that Josh had to step in front of her. Mrs. Sturdevant lagged behind too.

Chet and Danny looked at Josh hopelessly.

Wicked Warner was forced to lead the somber parade, and she looked for all the world like a pirate's captive walking the plank.

Outside, Josh saw a black van pulled up to the curb in front of the building. The motor was running. All he could see inside was the outline of a tall man.

The man evidently saw them, too, because he made an emphatic what's-going-on kind of gesture.

Josh gave it one last shot.

"Sure you can't stay and help us, Mrs. Warner?" he asked. His voice trembled so badly it embarrassed him.

Wicked Warner looked as if she desperately wanted to stay. She smiled sadly.

It was dusk. The sky grew darker, and the shadows lengthened. A weird, foreboding feeling hung heavy in the air. Dark clouds shifted in strange patterns.

But Warner always kept her word.

"Tomorrow, boys," she said. "But you go home and give the algebra a try. Remember, try to digest it in small bites."

Mrs. Sturdevant smiled and held open the door of the van. Wicked Warner got in. Gladys had already hopped in the back.

"Bye, Mrs. Warner! Take care!" Danny called, piercing the ominous stillness. Wicked Warner nodded.

The van rumbled away.

"What now?" Chet asked.

For the first time, Chet sounded halfway concerned, Josh thought.

"Go where they live?" Danny suggested. Chet nodded and looked at Josh.

Josh studied his shoes.

"Uh, guys," he stammered. "I have no *idea* where the Sturdevants live!"

Chapter Eighteen

Chet stared at Josh as if he were an alien.

"You mean to tell me you spend all this time with Michael Weirdo and you don't even know where the Weirdos live?" he asked.

Josh shook his head. It did seem surprising, actually.

"Well," said Chet, squinting down the road, "that van was speeding so fast, I didn't even see if it turned off somewhere. Did you?"

Josh shook his head again. So did Danny.

Chet was about to say something very rude. Josh knew the look. But they didn't have time for one of Chet's sulking sessions.

"What do you guys say we go back to my house and look up their address in the phone book," Josh said. He started walking.

"I still don't get why you don't know where the guy lives," Chet said, falling in stride beside Josh.

Danny followed.

Josh's mind reeled. If three guys left at five o'clock and ran one-eighth of a mile, but they didn't know which direction the van had gone, where would they be at six? Boy, Wicked Warner had certainly affected his brain in a serious way. Suddenly, he thought that if anything happened to her, he would miss her terribly.

Josh realized that if it hadn't been for being friends with Michael, he would never have cared so much about Wicked Warner.

What would have happened to her if he and Michael had never become friends?

The same thing, he supposed, that had happened to all the others.

*   *   *

"Earth to Josh. Earth to Josh," Chet said.

Josh was lost in his thoughts.

"I wonder how many other victims there have been." he muttered.

"Victims of what?" Chet asked. "I don't even know the point of this whole chase. I just know it's got me real worked up."

Josh was busy thinking. If he were not helping Michael right now, no one would be. Besides him, Michael had no friends at all.

Then he remembered. The other victims *were* the friends!

He began to tremble violently.

Chet grabbed his arm and tried to shake him out of it. Then Danny grabbed his other arm and shook even harder.

"Gone without a trace," Chet said.

"Who's gone without a trace?" Danny asked.

"Josh's mind," Chet said.

Panic spread in waves over Josh's body. His house was only two blocks away, but he could no longer even walk.

He sank down onto the curb.

"Remember those other people in our class who just stopped showing up at school?" he asked. "Who didn't get an intercom announcement like everyone else does, saying they were moving or their parents were yanking them into home schooling or whatever?"

Danny nodded.

"Three in our class, since I got here in second grade," he said.

"And lots of others in other classes," Josh said. He started trembling again, and he wrapped his arms around himself as if he were cold.

Chet and Danny looked at each other and rolled their eyes.

Chet shifted uneasily and scuffled his feet on the pavement.

"I think this has been a wild goose chase," he said. "Wicked Warner's fine. She's having a nice dinner with the weirdos and she'll be back tomorrow. Nothing strange happened to those kids. And speaking of dinner, I don't want to miss mine."

"I have to go too," Danny said.

Josh sighed. He couldn't force them to stay.

The boys parted at the end of the street, with Danny close on Chet's heels.

"You know my number, Josh my man," Chet said. "Any more teacher tricks, just holler."

"Bye," Danny said.

Chapter Nineteen

As Josh burst in the front door, Mrs. Jennings looked up with surprise from the sofa, where she sat hunched over her laptop computer.

She had decided last week that someone ought to be home when Josh and Megan came home from school. Mr. Jennings was working long hours at the office.

Mrs. Jennings had told everyone she was going to try to learn how to use the crock-pot, which slow-cooked food all day. But learning would take time, she cautioned.

"Josh, are you home early from practice or is my watch wrong?" she asked.

"Um, yes, we got out early, Mom," Josh called. He was already halfway up the stairs. "I'm up in my room, OK?"

"Any terrific test papers to show me?" Mrs. Jennings asked hopefully. "Nothing interesting at school? No snack? I have string cheese."

"No thanks, maybe in a while"

Josh sprinted up the rest of the stairs. On the way to his room he grabbed the phone book off the hall table.

He closed the door to his room behind him and sank into the black beanbag chair in the center of his room. He started thumbing through the phone book under "S."

Stevens, Stuart, Sturdevant.

"Yes!" he cried.

He lifted his red cellular telephone from its cradle perched on a stack of Soccer Today magazines. The phone had been a gift from Mr. Jennings, a reward for Josh's improved grades.

The phone rang five times before someone answered.

"Hello?"

It was the voice of a very young girl, nearly a baby. Not the raspy-voiced Gladys. Josh felt relieved.

But perhaps there was a younger version of Gladys in the household. A Gladys monster-baby?

The thought made him shiver.

"Hello, is this the Sturdevant residence?" Josh forced himself to ask.

"Who's calling?"

The baby was screening the call! She was smart, like them! But he didn't have time to worry about that.

"This is Josh. Josh Jennings."

"Do we know you?" the child demanded.

"Yes. No. Sort of. Look, just tell me if Michael is there, please?"

There was a pause on the other end.

"I think you're a stranger. I'm not allowed to talk to a stranger," the voice said. Then the baby hung up the phone with a loud click.

Josh redialed the number, praying someone other than that little girl would answer. If she did, he would try to disguise his voice, and just ask for her mother or something.

"Sturdevants'," a deep male voice answered.

Josh decided to play it more polite this time. "Hello, this is Josh Jennings. I'd like to speak to Michael Sturdevant, please."

"There's no Michael Sturdevant here," the man boomed jovially. "Just Bob, Jean and little Dottie Sturdevant."

"And you're the only Sturdevant in the book," Josh said, crestfallen.

"Yep, we're a rare breed," the man said. "Most of us live over there in Montana. But why don't you check information. There may be some we don't know about. Good-bye."

Click.

Josh dialed 411 and asked for a listing for Sturdevant.

"We have a Robert Sturdevant on Esau Street. Do you want that number?"

"No."

Bob, Jean and Little Dottie were definitely not the Sturdevants he was seeking. Esau Street was across town. Not even in the same school district.

"There are no others?" His voice sounded whiny, even to himself.

"Well, there *is* one other Sturdevant, but that one is unlisted."

"Can you just give me a street name then?" Josh pleaded.

"I'm sorry, that information is not available," the operator said pleasantly.

Click.

Dang it! Josh slammed down the phone.

How would he find Michael's house? What was Wicked Warner doing now? What were the Sturdevants doing?

Sweat trickled down his forehead. He mopped his brow with his shirt.

He stole a glance at the digital clock by his bed.

It showed 6:06 p.m. He let out a sigh. It was not dinner time yet.

Was it?

Chapter Twenty

Why in the world, Josh wondered, hadn't he asked Michael when the Sturdevants ate dinner?

He needed to know. Because, he knew, with a wrenching feeling in his stomach, that this had everything to do with dinner.

He knew, though, why he had not asked. He hadn't really wanted to know.

Still, why hadn't Michael tossed him another hint? He had said he wanted Josh's help, and then he'd left him with hardly any clues. No time, no directions, no phone number, no address.

"What the heck do I do now?" Josh asked himself aloud.

He scrunched down in his beanbag chair and flipped through one of his soccer magazines without really looking at the pages.

His mother would grill him if he asked her what to do. She would probably do something legal, like suing. Josh imagined Michael wearing a Pilgrim hat with a big buckle on the front, on the witness stand with his wrists shackled together, pointing at Gladys, who sat sandwiched at the defense table between two lumpy lawyers, who also wore Pilgrim hats.

No, that would definitely not do.

How would he make it through the night with all these things rattling around in his head?

He reached for his backpack and pulled out his portable chess set to distract himself. He unwrapped the cedar box that held the chessmen, lifted the lid, inhaled the woodsy smell and fingered the black and white pieces.

Then, under the pieces, he spotted a yellow slip of paper.

He grabbed a corner and pulled it out. It was covered with black, spidery writing. A note!

JOSH: NOW THAT MRS. WARNER'S HERE, THERE'S NOTHING MORE TO DO. FOR NOW. DO NOT COME HERE. IT WON'T HELP. GIVING YOU MY ADDRESS WOULD ONLY IMPERIL YOU.

THANKS FOR TRYING TO STOP HER. I HAVE NEVER BEEN ABLE TO STOP ANYONE. BUT I'LL TRY MY BEST TO STOP WHAT WILL HAPPEN HERE. I'M GOING TO TRY TO CALL YOU LATER.

THINK ABOUT ME, WILL YA, MAN?
YOUR FRIEND, MICHAEL.

Josh stared at the paper. Too late to do anything?

Michael had to have written this note before school was out. He must have known their efforts to stop Wicked Warner would fail.

And Michael would try his best to stop what *will* happen? He must not have much faith in his own efforts!

Here was Michael, a straight-A student with a brilliant strategy for every chess move. And he didn't think he could stop it.

If Michael had not been able to save the others, how could Josh save Wicked Warner?

But Michael *was* trying. At least his note said that much.

Josh promised himself he would help, too, once he got the word. It terrified him, but he would help.

The buzz of the hall intercom interrupted his thoughts.

"Josh! Dinner! Time to eat!"

He jumped a foot out of the chair. And he didn't think he was hungry at all.

Chapter Twenty-One

When he reached the kitchen, Mrs. Jennings was leaning over the kitchen island, nervously drumming her fingers and staring at the crock-pot.

"I buzzed too soon," she said miserably. "The crock-pot is still practically freezing. It was just going to be you and me for dinner, and I was making Hearty Beef Stew."

"Uh, how long did you cook — um, the stew?"

"Forty minutes," Mrs. Jennings said. "I thought that was long enough. My mother always seemed to pretty much whip it together on the stove."

Josh sighed.

"Mom, you cook things all day in a crock-pot."

"Well, maybe if I cook it through the night you and Megan can take it to school tomorrow for lunch. A nice homemade lunch. How would that be?"

She looked so unhappy that Josh felt sorry for her.

"That would be just great, Mom," he said. "I'm sure all the other kids would be jealous."

Mrs. Jennings perked up. She went over to pat the crock-pot.

"Do you really think so?" she asked. "Well, good. I'm glad you like that idea. Next time I'll start our evening meal at breakfast-time. So," she said, throwing open the freezer door, "what'll it be, soldier?"

"I'm not very hungry, to tell the truth," Josh said. "Where are Megan and Dad?"

"Megan's with Heidi, studying, and your dad is on deadline."

Mrs. Jennings opened the cupboard and grabbed two cans of chunky soup.

"Actually, I'm glad it's just you and me," she said, "because I have something I want to discuss with you."

Josh pulled up a kitchen stool and gave his mother the most innocent look he could muster.

"What do you know about Michael Sturdevant's parents?" Mrs. Jennings asked.

Josh had no idea what to say. So he said, "Huh?"

He brushed his bangs out of his eyes and tried to look even more innocent.

"I know you kids feel his sister is odd, but that happens in families," Mrs. Jennings said. "And Michael is such a nice boy. Although very hungry. What I want to know is, what kind of parents does he have."

Josh stared at her as she set two steaming bowls of soup on the kitchen counter and pulled up a stool. She handed him a spoon.

She did not look worried, Josh saw, nor even mildly concerned. Just interested.

"Why do you want to know?" he asked.

Mrs. Jennings' eyebrows shot up.

"Well, that was direct," she said. "Your father and I are driving to my high school reunion in Bainsville Friday night, and I've decided I'd like to spend the night and come back the next day."

"But why can't I — "

"You cannot stay here alone with Megan. What if something were to happen?"

They'd had this conversation a thousand times.

"Anyway," Mrs. Jennings went on, "I thought since you and Michael spend so much time together, and he's such a nice influence, maybe you could stay with the Sturdevants, and Megan can stay with Heidi. But I don't know the Sturdevants, so I'm not sure I'm comfortable with that."

Josh gasped.

He had no desire to go there for dinner —
much less stay overnight!

Chapter Twenty-Two

"Josh, you're pale! Is something wrong?"

Mrs. Jennings clamped her palm on Josh's forehead.

Josh shook his head vigorously, mostly to get rid of the image of staying overnight at the Sturdevants'.

"I don't know where they live," he said, finally.

Boy, was that ever the truth.

Mrs. Jennings shrugged.

"You're right. I don't think that it's a good idea. Perhaps you can stay with Chet. Why don't you ask him about it tomorrow, and let me know? I know we can arrange something. You have so many friends."

Josh's body was numb. All he could do was nod.

Mrs. Jennings put their bowls in the dishwasher and went to her study.

Josh shuffled back to his room. He was totally freaked by his mother's proposal — him, stay with the Sturdevants for a whole night? He had gotten out of it quite easily, but just the idea terrified him.

He flopped on his bed and picked up Michael's note.

He read the words again: *AND GIVING YOU MY ADDRESS WOULD IMPERIL YOU.*

No, not the kind of place he wanted to spend the night.

He grabbed his soccer ball from the floor and bounced it against the wall. This was against his mom's rules, but dang it, he'd never been so nervous.

Breeeng!

Hands shaking, Josh dropped the soccer ball and grabbed the phone.

"Jennings, my man!" said Chet. "Guess where I'm going this weekend?"

Josh was speechless.

"Jennings, you flake, are you there?"

"Uh, so where you going?" Josh asked.

"Five-Star Pro-Wrestling Tour with Stylin' Steve. It's at the Moxie. It's sold out!"

"Sold out? How'd you rig that up?"

"Danny," Chet answered sheepishly. "He got tickets from his cousin who works for the show. Danny doesn't have a father you know, and his mom

74

hates wrestling — says it's fake and all that. So my dad's gonna take us. Too bad there wasn't another ticket — you could have gone."

"Listen," Josh said, "I can't tie up the phone. So, uh, guess that means you guys won't be around to help me if I need it on Friday night."

"Help on Friday?"

"Yeah, just in case. Remember what we did today?"

"Oh" Chet said. "I thought by Friday whatever was gonna happen would have happened."

Actually, Josh thought to himself, Chet was right.

He gulped.

"Well, gotta go. See you tomorrow."

"See you."

Josh hung up. Then he raised the receiver again to see if any other messages had come in while he was talking to Chet.

There were two. The first was from Megan, who wanted somebody to pick her up because she and Heidi had had an argument.

Impatiently, Josh saved Megan's message so he could hear the second one.

It was Michael. He spoke rapidly, in a hushed tone.

"Josh, it's urgent, man. I'll call back if I can. Try to keep the phone clear, *please*! I may not be able to get to the phone again."

Chapter Twenty-Three

Josh waited for the phone to ring again.

And waited, and waited.

His clock read 9 o'clock.

Breeng!

He grabbed the phone.

"Yes!" he screamed, realizing for the first time how overwrought he had become.

"Josh, it's me," Michael said softly.

"What's going on!" Josh demanded, lowering his voice to a harsh whisper. He sat up straight on his bed and grabbed Michael's yellow note. "How is Wicked Warner?"

"Um, OK, at least sort of — for another couple of days, I figure. It happens. But — "

"What happens!"

Michael sighed.

"I can't go into all of it now. What I'm trying to say is, she's all right for the time being. But" — his voice dropped low again — "uh, listen, remember I told you I don't want you over here? It's dangerous, like I said. But the only way I can save Mrs. Warner is with your help. You're athletic, and you're smart. I don't have anybody else, Josh. I'm desperate."

"What? Tell me what's going on, man!"

Josh had never been so worked up in his life.

He caught his breath. The compliments calmed him some.

"Listen," he said. "I can come over. My mom needs me to stay over at somebody's Friday night. Just me, not Megan."

So Wicked Warner was still OK. Maybe he *could* do something.

"That would be fantastic man," Michael said. "I'll try and help keep you as safe as I can. Because I don't want to lose you as . . . my . . . my friend. And I like Mrs. Warner, too."

Michael paused for a moment, and Josh thought he heard the sounds of snuffling.

"Josh," Michael said finally. "I can't stand to lose anyone else I like!"

"Uh, Mike, take it easy," Josh pleaded. Michael was making him nervous again. "But, uh, my mom won't buy this right now because she doesn't know your folks. What can we do about that?"

Silence.

"Well, I guess she'll need a reference," Michael said.

"Who in the heck would that be? Who knows your family that my mom would trust?"

"How about Mrs. Warner?"

*   *   *

Wicked Warner was not in class the next day.

Of course, Josh was not surprised.

They had a substitute, Ms. French, who claimed she "lived for algebra." She was so old she made Warner look like a teen-ager.

Everyone in the class speculated about where Wicked Warner was, because she had never once missed school. Josh tried to ignore the whisperings.

He was so tired he almost had to prop himself up in his chair at lunch. He had barely slept ten minutes last night, worrying about the mission he'd taken on.

And Megan had gotten on his nerves when she carped at him for about half an hour for forgetting to tell their mother she wanted to get picked up.

Heidi had been "completely abominable," Megan said. She'd been stuck at Heidi's for an extra hour while she waited for someone to call her back.

But Heidi was at their house this morning, as always, waiting for Megan to walk to school with her.

Josh had no idea how he could make it through the rest of the school day. And then soccer practice?

"I can get my cellular phone to Mrs. Warner, I think," Michael told him.

No chessboard lay between them today. Michael's voice faded in and out of Josh's weary brain.

"She can call your mom and tell her how terrific my family is. She'll have to lie, of course. Will your mom buy a reference coming from a teacher?"

"Yes, I'm pretty sure she would," Josh said.

He waited a few moments before asking the question that had bugged him for most of his restless night.

"Mike, why did you put that note in my chess box, knowing we wouldn't be able to stop her from going over there?"

Chapter Twenty-Four

Michael didn't answer immediately. Then he looked up.

"Because I knew they'd win. They always do. But we had to try, and I didn't want you to feel bad. Plus, you had to know I was gonna try to call."

Josh stared at the empty table.

"So do you think they'll win this time?"

Michael averted his eyes a moment. Then he looked back at Josh with new determination.

"No," he said. "Not unless it happens tonight instead."

"Why not?"

"Because I have competent help."

Josh was flattered, and the compliment made him feel a little less scared.

"I'll do my best," he said. "But Chet and Danny are going to a wrestling match. They won't be able to help me."

"That's just as well. Too many people would — well, my parents would be just like kids in a candy store. And Gladys would be the kid with the money."

Michael smiled cryptically.

"Danny just copies what Chet does," he said. "And Chet has a tendency to botch things, pardon my candor. He's the one who wrecked the plans to detain Mrs. Warner yesterday."

"Who told you about that?"

"Mrs. Warner."

"When did she say that?"

"Uh, after they locked her up — "

"*Locked her up*?"

Fear shot through Josh's body.

"Better than the alternative," Michael said. "Make no bones about it."

Chapter Twenty-Five

Soccer practice whirled around Josh. He didn't even feel like he was really there.

It was his worse practice ever. He could barely stand up, much less run or kick a ball. Everybody kept yelling, "Get the lead out!" and "What's with you, Jennings?"

He couldn't wait to go home, up to his room, and collapse. If he could climb the stairs.

But when he got there, his mom flagged him down from the sofa.

"Yes, Mom?" he managed to say wanly.

He noticed the crock-pot bubbling merrily on the counter. He wondered how many minutes it'd been on this time.

"I received the loveliest call today from your math teacher, Mary Warner."

"Oo-ee," Megan said from the sofa, where she was assembling a new school organizer. "Teachers are calling you at home now?"

Mary? Josh thought. Wicked Warner's first name was Mary? He had never considered that Wicked Warner might have a first name. Other than Wicked.

"She sounded so tired," Mrs. Jennings said. "I asked her about it, she said she had lots of grading to do. And she said you had done so well, and she was so proud of you. I told her, of course, we couldn't be more pleased."

She stopped to beam at Josh a moment.

"Anyway," she went on, "she said the Sturdevants are very friendly. And they *love* other people. She said when she met them, they swept her off her feet at once. So I feel good about having you stay over there Friday night."

"What?" Megan yelped, yanking her head up from the organizer. "Josh is staying at the Sturdevants'? What, are you crazy, Mom?"

"And how," Josh muttered under his breath. But he felt like *he* was really the crazy one.

"Well great, Mom, thanks," he said.

Mrs. Jennings peered at him.

"Josh, you look exhausted! Was practice all right?"

"Mom!" Megan demanded. "I mean, have you seen these weird people?"

"Have *you*?" Josh retorted.

That shut Megan up.

"I'm OK," Josh said. "I just need to lie down a while."

"Well, if you're sure you're feeling all right," Mrs. Jennings said. "Let me get you a glass of water to take up with you."

"Thanks."

Josh dragged himself upstairs, barely able to hold the glass. When he reached his room, he closed the door, collapsed on his bed, and immediately fell asleep in his soccer clothes.

Chapter Twenty-Six

And then it was Friday morning.

Josh had arrived at school early to meet Michael in front of the cafeteria. He had slept through supper the night before, waking only for a midnight snack.

He was glad he'd gotten all that sleep. He didn't expect to get much tonight. This was the night he'd be going to the Sturdevants' home.

The home of Gladys. And that creepy Mrs. Sturdevant.

"I could just eat you up!" she'd said. Nope, no sleep tonight.

"Wicked Warner called my mom," Josh told Michael. "My mom thinks the whole thing is just ducky now."

"Good. My mom doesn't know a thing. I'm just going to pop you on her, so she won't have time to plan anything. Catch her off guard, you know. It's good that she's one of these indecisive types."

Josh had stashed a change of clothes, pajamas and a toothbrush in his gym bag. He didn't plan to use the pajamas, though. He didn't plan to shut one eye the entire time, not even to blink.

"Did you bring your chess stuff?" Michael asked him.

"Yeah." Josh patted the angular bulge in his green nylon bag.

Just then, Megan rushed up, breathless. Her eyes bulged in disbelief.

"Heidi's mom is sick!" she cried.

"So Heidi can't make it to school?" Josh asked. "And that's supposed to be bad?"

"I don't know why you're so mean to her. Especially since her mother's sick and all," Megan said.

Then her eyes widened again with worry.

"I can't stay over at Heidi's tonight," she said miserably.

"So, what does that mean? Where are you gonna stay?" Josh asked. He was beginning to worry.

Megan looked fearfully at Michael, then back at Josh.

"At the Sturdevants', Mom said."

Chapter Twenty-Seven

Oh, great. This was a riot, Josh thought grimly.

Ms. French rattled through the algebra lesson. Josh had no idea what she was talking about.

Megan was coming, too? How could he keep her out of the way while he and Michael rescued Wicked Warner?

Megan wasn't his favorite person — far from it — but he had to look after her. He couldn't allow her to disappear like the others.

He thought about it all day, but he could not come up with any way to keep Megan from coming to the Sturdevants'. He still had no plan when he met her in front of the Thomas J. Media Center after school. Heidi stood beside Megan and looked almost as worried — which was something, considering that she usually portrayed herself as superior to everyone else in the universe.

"What is *she* doing here," Josh demanded.

"Her mother's at the hospital," Megan whined. "She has appendicitis. Heidi has to come with us."

Josh shook his head back and forth vehemently.

"No way," he said. "It's bad enough you have to come. Heidi can't just walk in to the Sturdevants' and say, 'Here I am.'"

"Well, technically she could," said Michael, out of nowhere. "But I wouldn't advise it."

Josh whirled around, startled. He hadn't heard Michael come up.

"My mother's too sick to make arrangements for me for the night," Heidi said. "And I don't have anyone else to go home with."

"Yeah, I wonder why," Josh muttered.

Heidi stayed silent. Usually she'd have responded with some cutting remark or other.

"Well, I don't know," Josh said hesitantly.

"We have an awful lot of cooks in the kitchen now," Michael said. "I know my parents won't mind more guests. The more the merrier, they say."

He looked uneasily at Josh.

"Actually," he said, gloomily, "that's what I'm afraid of."

But there was no alternative. At least Josh couldn't think of one.

"How are we going to get to the Sturdevants'?" Megan whined.

She still did not address Michael directly. She did not even look at him.

"We walk," said Michael. "I don't live far from here. You'd be amazed at how close it is."

"I never walk in the smog," Heidi announced. Her conceit was showing again.

Michael thought he knew how to handle Heidi.

"Well, in this case, riding would be your worst mistake," he said. "You see, you would have to ride in my parents' van."

"Why can't your parents pick us up? Someone *always* picks me up."

Josh was fed up.

"Heidi, you don't understand," he shouted.

But why would she? She hadn't been here to see Wicked Warner get carted off in that awful van.

"We're walking," Josh said, "and you don't know how lucky you are."

Heidi stuck out her tongue at him.

"Josh, you'd better be nice to Heidi," Megan warned. "She's worried about her mother."

And I, Josh thought, am worried about all the rest of us.

Chapter Twenty-Eight

Following Michael, the group walked in a direction that took them away from the neighborhood where everyone else in school lived.

After just a few blocks, Michael paused.

"We're just about there," he said. "Now, I need to brief you all."

"Hey, where are we?" Heidi asked. "I've never been on this street."

"My mom does briefs all the time," Megan said. "Legal briefs."

Josh wished Megan and Heidi would quit their prattling. They were really getting on his nerves now — and he was uptight enough.

"Should we tell them, Josh?" asked Michael. "Only you know what they can handle."

Michael shoved his hand in the pockets of his jeans and looked at Josh anxiously.

Josh had been too chicken himself to hear absolutely everything — although he was pretty sure he'd guessed the rest, anyway. Maybe they could give the girls a hint, just so they knew to be on the lookout.

Suddenly, they saw the black van. It was parked, half concealed by leafy branches, on a driveway that sloped steeply into a small valley.

At the foot of the driveway Josh could make out a large stone house. It, too, was nearly hidden behind gnarled, leafy trees and deep green ivy. What would his mom call it, an English Tudor?

It wasn't an ugly house, at any rate. But it was a hidden one, looking almost as if it had been concealed on purpose.

Those ditzy girls needed to be aware they were in danger. On the other hand, scaring them to death might make them too nervous to function.

Josh realized that Michael did not have younger-sister problems like this. His younger sister was Gladys.

Josh decided he had to tell Megan and Heidi something.

"You know how everyone's afraid of Gladys?" he began.

"And him too," Heidi said, pointing perfectly obviously at Michael.

Heidi was so tactless — but there was no time to hate her right now.

"Well Michael's a friend," Josh said. "Gladys is not."

He hesitated.

"Uh, Mike, can I say your parents aren't safe either?" he asked. He was suddenly worried he would offend Michael. They were, after all, his parents.

But Michael was not offended at all.

"Stay away from them all!" he said.

Worry lines creased Megan's forehead. Her eyes widened with fear.

"Why are we staying here?" she cried.

They heard a squeaking coming up the driveway.

A hot-pink mountain bike wobbled towards them. It was being pedaled up the nearly vertical driveway by a person wearing hobnailed boots.

Slowly, Gladys emerged into full view. Megan and Heidi stumbled back at the sight of her.

Gladys hopped off her bike and let it fall with a crash. She stood there and ogled them for a moment.

"Company!" she yelled.

She rushed up to them and clasped her plump little hands to her chest.

"Have they come to dinner?" she asked

"No," Michael said firmly. "They're guests. Mine."

"'I'm going to tell Mom!" Gladys grinned.

She ran back down the driveway toward the house, her stumpy pigtails flying behind her. Halfway down the driveway, she turned and looked lingeringly at Josh.

Even at that distance, he thought he saw her pink tongue flicker across her lips.

Michael turned to them.

"Well guys, this is it," he said. "One word of caution: Don't turn your back on her. Or anyone."

"Why?" Megan whimpered.

Heidi was quiet. Then she nodded slowly, as if she had figured something out.

"Meg, let's you and me hang out outside a while," she said softly. Josh had always disliked Heidi, but he'd never said she was stupid.

Michael smiled.

"Excellent idea," he said. "That's probably the best thing you could do. I hate it that you all got dragged into this."

Then his face turned grim.

"I know how people can never stay away from places they're told to stay away from," he said. "But, *please* — stay away from that stone carriage house in back."

Megan was about to ask another question, but Josh interrupted her.

"I'll be back to check on you in a while," he said. He began walking briskly toward the house.

Michael caught up with him quickly.

"Guess you're ready to face what has to be faced," he said.

When they reached the front steps, Josh turned back to look up at the street. He could barely see it through the heavy brambles.

He turned back to the front door. He could see no numbers on it.

Before he could get his thoughts together, someone inside the house whisked open the door.

Chapter Twenty-Nine

"My dear!" Mrs. Sturdevant exclaimed.

She wore the same dowdy green dress. She clasped her hands to her chest in delight, just as Gladys had done.

"My, my," she said. "This is the nice big boy we saw the other day at school."

She grabbed Josh's arm — she had a surprisingly strong grip — and pulled him into the foyer.

It was freezing in the house. Mrs. Sturdevant's eager eyes never left Josh. She looked him up and down appreciatively.

"Can I get you anything?" she asked, without relaxing her grip on his arm. "Coffee? Tea? Or me?" she chuckled.

Josh felt sick.

"He's just a guest, Mom," Michael said warily.

Mrs. Sturdevant ignored her son.

"Uh, could I have a glass of water?" Josh asked.

He glanced at Michael. Michael nodded. The water must be safe to drink. Josh was relieved, because his mouth felt as dry as sand.

"Come with me to the kitchen while I fix it, and we'll step outside into the back garden for a moment. I'll show you my herbs," Mrs. Sturdevant said, yanking Josh along with her. It sounded like an order rather than an invitation.

Out of the corner of his eye, Josh saw Michael slowly shaking his head. No, he was saying.

Josh grabbed hold of the post at the foot of the stairs to keep from being dragged along by Mrs. Sturdevant.

"Uh, no thanks, I'll just stay here."

Mrs. Sturdevant looked deeply disappointed.

"Well, all right," she said. "Why don't you boys go to the family room and have a seat. Or, better yet, why don't you visit Gladdy's room?"

Hope sprang back into her eyes.

"No, Mom," Michael said sharply.

Josh was shaken. His heart raced. He had practically had to fight her off!

Chapter Thirty

Without a word, Josh followed Michael into the living room.

Photographs of all shapes and sizes covered the walls. They were mounted in all kinds of different frames — some ornate, others plain, some of metal, others of wood. They showed all manner of people — fat, thin, old, young, and middle-aged.

Some of the pictures looked old-fashioned, in the red-brown sepia tones of Civil War photographs. Others, slightly more recent, were in black and white. Others were newer still, in full color.

Some of the pictures appeared to be formal portraits. Others were only snapshots, but they too were framed. There were even a couple of eight-by-ten school pictures.

Josh tried to think of something to say.

"These your family?" he asked.

He shivered. The cold air was getting to him. So were the pictures. They unsettled him.

"Uh, no, just friends, I guess you could say," Michael said. He settled awkwardly into a chair.

Josh sat down across from Michael. He didn't want to get too comfortable; it'd make him sleepy. He was already worn out with worry.

He stared again at the photographs. A school portrait caught his eye. The boy's face looked familiar.

In a flash of horror he knew who it was.

Billy Johns!

The boy who had disappeared from school almost two years ago.

Michael cleared his throat.

"Shall we go to my room and play a game of chess?" he asked. "Clear the cobwebs, get our heads together? And my room looks out on the side yard. We can watch Megan and Heidi from up there."

Josh wished with all his might that he had never come here. But it was too late.

Wicked Warner's safety was at stake. And so was his — and Megan's, and Heidi's.

"Uh, sure man," Josh said, forcing himself to tear his eyes from the face of Billy Johns.

Nothing in the world could make him ask why that picture was on the wall. He knew he could never bear to hear the answer.

*　　*　　*

Michael's room seemed like a normal kid's room.

For starters, it was warmer than the rest of the house. And there were no photos on the wall, only posters. A computer sat on a desk.

Of course, normal was a relative term. The posters weren't exactly *cool* posters. They were *brain* posters — like a diagram of the solar system, and another of a particular ecosystem.

Michael liked living things. Josh was glad of that.

Josh walked over to the huge window across the room. A table under it held a beautiful chess set. He peered out the window.

"Oh, I can see Megan and Heidi now," he said with relief.

The girls were sitting in the grass, rummaging through their backpacks. Probably getting ready to have a showdown about who had the better homework paper.

Even from this high up, Josh could tell they weren't their usual ditzy, unconcerned selves. They seemed solemn. Both sat facing the house, and they kept glancing around.

Josh craned his neck to see the driveway.

The van was gone.

Chapter Thirty-One

"Chess?" asked Michael.

Josh nodded numbly. He had to do something to ease the tension. Worry would only sap his strength, and he had to be in good form tonight.

Josh took the white pieces, as usual. The first move was his. He put his finger to his lips and pondered.

"Uh, where's your dad?" he asked. "The van's gone."

"Oh, probably gone to get some take-out," Michael said. So, Josh thought, Mr. Sturdevant had been driving the van that day at school.

Focus on the game, Josh told himself. Concentrate.

Only few seconds later, it seemed, he looked at his watch. Forty minutes had passed!

"Check," said Michael.

Speaking of checking, where were Megan and Heidi?

Josh turned to the window and looked into the yard. Dusk cast long shadows across it, creating pockets of gloom and darkness.

Megan and Heidi were gone!

Their backpacks lay in the grass. The girls were nowhere in sight.

Josh gasped. A look of terror crossed his face. He tried to speak, but only gurgled.

"What's wrong, man?" Michael asked.

"Megan and Heidi are gone!" Josh blurted out.

Michael jumped up and ran to the window.

"I really thought it was better for them to be outside, keep them away from Gladys," he said. "She almost never goes out there, except to ride her bike."

Michael sounded alarmed. He craned his neck to see the driveway.

"Her bike is still there," he said.

Josh looked. The bike lay on its side in the driveway where Gladys had ditched it earlier. But where were the girls?

Josh's throat felt tight. It occurred to him that Megan was a pretty good little sister — and even Heidi wasn't really such a bad person.

"I'll bet anything Gladys is in her room, and they're with her," Michael said. "Come on."

Down the chilly upstairs hall they walked, until they came to the last door on the right. A cardboard sign in crooked lettering hung from the doorknob: "Gladdy's room. No trespassing."

Michael pushed open the door.

"Mi-*chael*!" Gladys shrieked. "You're supposed to knock!"

She sat in the middle of the room, which was bare except for a cot and a hard-backed wood chair.

She was alone.

In each hand, she held a hairless doll that had seen better days.

"We're having a dinner party," she said, turning the ragged dolls toward Josh and Michael, chortling.

Josh noticed there were pictures on her walls, too, more sparse than those downstairs, but the same hodgepodge of people — young, old, fat, thin. These photos, however, looked newer. All were in color; the people wore more up-to-date styles.

Who *were* these people?

Suddenly, Josh spotted another familiar face. A young girl with blond hair in ponytails.

Bessie Butler. From the bus. The girl Megan had always watched.

The girl who had also disappeared.

Chapter Thirty-Two

"Well, they're not here," Michael said. "We've got to get outside."

Josh followed him out of Gladys's room, glad to get out of it.

His heart throbbed in his throat. Terror flowed in his veins.

They *had* to find Megan and Heidi. Fast. He couldn't bear to lose his sister!

They clambered down the stairs, past another photo gallery on the stairwell.

Michael yanked open the front door.

"Mi-*chael*!" Mrs. Sturdevant's voice called from the back of the house. "Bring that big boy in here a minute."

"Go ahead, Mike," Josh whispered. "Please! See if you can find Megan and Heidi before anything happens! I'll be OK."

Josh felt that something was drawing him back toward the kitchen. He couldn't believe he'd just told Michael to leave him alone in that house.

"Trust me, I'll find them," Michael said. "Dad's not around, and Gladys is upstairs, so I *think* you'll be OK. Just keep your back to the wall, then duck out the back door."

*   *   *

Mrs. Sturdevant stood in the kitchen, boiling water in a yellow kettle.

"Would you like a brisk cup of tea, nice big boy?" she asked.

Yikes, why did she call him that?

"It's Josh," Josh said. "No thanks."

"Not a spot of tea?"

She poured steaming water into a pink flowered teacup and heaped in four spoonfuls of brown sugar.

"Low blood sugar," she explained, and looked up at Josh with that overly pleasant expression of hers. "What blood type are you?"

Josh kept his back to the wall. He glanced at the door. Just a few feet away.

"Uh," he stammered. "D-minus, I think."

Mrs. Sturdevant turned back to the stove.

"Well, I need to go find Michael," Josh said in as chipper a manner as he could manage.

Mrs. Sturdevant, preoccupied with something, did not respond right away.

Josh stepped quickly to the back door.

As he fumbled with the greasy doorknob, a photograph thumbtacked beside the door caught his eye.

It was a snapshot of a boy on a soccer field. He was standing sideways, looking down the field, wearing a number 12 soccer jersey.

Josh gasped.

It was a photo of himself!

Chapter Thirty-Three

From the look of it, the photo had been taken during a soccer game.

Their last real game had been last fall! Had they had their eyes on him that long ago?

"Excuse me," Josh stammered. He started to shake.

He pulled again at the slippery doorknob — it was unlocked, thank heavens! — and dashed into the yard, into the warmth of the late afternoon.

"Nice big boy!" Mrs. Sturdevant yelled after him. "Come back!"

What was going on here? Someone had obviously decided long ago that he would come here. He hadn't even *met* Gladys then, or creepy Mrs. Sturdevant, either. The only one in that family he'd known was . . . Michael.

Had Michael been working all this time to lure him to this evil house?

Gotta find them, gotta find them, Josh chanted to himself.

He rushed around the yard, looking behind trees and bushes and around corners.

He could not find them anywhere.

The van was still gone. The bike was still there.

He looked up and saw, with a start, that the door to the stone carriage house was ajar. Michael had emphatically told the girls it was off limits.

But now his thoughts about Michael were changing.

Could it be that Michael really *did* want them to go in the carriage house, and had known full well that his warning would only tempt them to do so?

*   *   *

Josh blinked in the dark doorway of the little house.

"Hello?" he whispered into the darkness.

No answer.

He cracked the door wider. Light hit some mossy flagstones. He stepped inside.

"Who's here?" he called. His voice echoed against the stones.

108

He froze. What if some Sturdevant was in here?

Suddenly, a hand reached out from the blackness and grabbed his arm!

"Aaaaah!"

The scream scared him badly. Who was it?

Then he realized the scream had been his own.

"Shh!" a voice whispered. "It's Heidi!"

Josh spun around, breaking the hand's grip on his arm. He could barely see the dim form standing next to him. But he recognized the voice. He'd always despised Heidi's high, irritating twang, but he was glad to hear it now.

"What are you doing, Heidi?" he hissed. "Where's Megan?"

"Michael told me to hide here," Heidi said. "I'm supposed to keep watch for Gladys or her parents. Megan's down there with Michael."

"Down where?" Josh cried. Michael, he felt, was just another enemy now.

"Down those steps in the cellar," Heidi said.

Josh's eyes were beginning to adjust to the darkness. Still, he could barely make out the stairs to which Heidi pointed.

"We were sitting in the yard," Heidi said. "And then we heard all this knocking coming from here in the carriage house. We thought we heard someone yelling 'Help! Help!'"

"You were not supposed to come in here!" Josh yelled.

"Josh, wouldn't you have checked on somebody who was yelling help?"

Yes. He knew he would have. When you came right down to it, checking on someone in the carriage house was what he himself was doing now.

But what if the yelling was a lure, a trap?

He had no time to think.

"I have to go down there," he said. "Keep watch for any other family members. If I don't come back, try to go get help. I'll try to yell up to you."

"OK," Heidi said.

She did not seem nearly as scared as she should have been.

Chapter Thirty-Four

All sorts of sounds echoed up from the bottom of the stairs.

Josh heard the clanging of metal. A voice said "Shoot!" every now and then. Then Josh heard Michael yell, "This dang thing!"

"You broke it!" Megan's voice wailed in anguish. "Mom'll kill me!"

"Megan!" Josh shouted. "Where are you!"

He scrambled down the stairs in the darkness. He couldn't find a banister railing, nor could he find a wall to guide him down the steep steps. He could see nothing. His feet tripped down the steps until they struck a level stone floor.

A beam of light clicked on and shone on his face.

"Shhh, Josh, she's fine," Michael said.

Josh blinked and looked around at the dark cellar. The flashlight cast a vague light around the gloomy room. Megan sat forlornly on a wooden crate.

Josh saw Michael fiddling with something on the front of what appeared to be a jail cell.

He was going to lock her up!

Josh rushed over and grabbed his sister by the shoulders.

"Megan, are you all right?" he said. "Why did you come in here?"

He turned around and glared at Michael.

"Stay away, man!" he shouted.

"What, it's not like *I'm* the one in trouble," Megan said, turning around and shooting him an embarrassed look. She brushed the loose hair out of her face.

"What?" Josh asked. He was totally baffled. Maybe he was losing his mind.

Michael muttered to himself, still fiddling with the door of the . . . heck, it was a cage!

"*I'm* the one in trouble, I'm afraid," another voice said. "I declare, if two children tried to help me in a cellar that was twenty-four feet deep, and a third child came to help them, how long would it take to get a poor math teacher out of here?"

Wicked Warner!

She sat wearing her prim blue suit in the middle of a huge cage, which was as big as a small room. Plates of uneaten dinners littered the cage. Well, at least they fed her, Josh thought. She was a bit thin.

Then a horrible thought occurred to him. Were they trying to fatten her up?

He heard metal grinding, and then a popping sound. He jumped.

"Hallelujah!" Michael cried. "I did it!"

The cage door slowly swung open.

"Megan's barrette worked," Michael said. "It actually picked that triple-duty lock. Thank you, Megan."

Chapter Thirty-Five

"Can I please have my Mexico barrette back now?" Megan asked.

Michael handed it to her.

"Yuck," she said. She wiped in on her jeans and clamped it back in her hair.

Wicked Warner stepped out of the cage and stood beside them, looking shaky. "Let's blow this Popsicle stand," she said.

"I didn't have the key," Michael explained to Josh. "But Megan offered her barrette. I never really understood what hair clips were for — until now."

"You're welcome," Megan said.

A shriek rang out from upstairs.

"She's coming!" Heidi screamed. "She's coming!"

"Who's coming?" Josh, Megan and Wicked Warner yelled together.

"We gotta run for it!" Michael said. "We can't get caught down here!"

Josh took the stairs two at a time. He reached the top first. He would lead them out of there as fast as he could.

"Josh! Watch out!" he heard Heidi yell.

Thwump! Sharp pain seared the back of his neck.

Then everything went black.

Chapter Thirty-Six

"Josh! Josh!"

It felt like a dream. Days must have passed. Josh felt groggy and wondered if he really *had* been dreaming. Where was he?

"Josh!"

He opened his eyes and found himself looking at a blurry round object. His focus sharpened. It was Heidi.

This *was* a nightmare, he decided.

"Josh, are you OK!" Heidi asked. She looked concerned.

"What happened?" he asked, his lips seeming to move in slow motion. He tried to move his arms, but he felt like a robot. He sat up slowly, with Heidi pulling on his arm to help him, and looked around.

Staring anxiously at him were Megan, Wicked Warner, and Michael.

"Gladys crowned you with one of her boots," Megan said.

116

"Man, I thought you were a goner," said Michael. "You must be a very hardy guy. But we've got to get you people out of here."

"Heidi got Gladys in a headlock as soon as she hit you," Megan said. "She held her until we could get upstairs. I really think you should thank Heidi for all she did."

"Then we put Gladys away for safekeeping," Michael finished.

Bars rattled downstairs; Josh could hear them now.

"Mi-*chael*!" a shrill voice screamed. "Let me out! It's almost time for dinner!"

Michael pulled Josh to his feet and said, "Let's get you guys out of here before Gladys gets out of that cage. She's strong. She has ways. And," he added, "I'm eternally grateful to you. I think you're brilliant, Josh my man."

*　　*　　*

Once they reached the road, Josh felt his sore limbs relax. The blood started circulating in his body again.

"Uh, Heidi," Josh said, not knowing quite how to say what he wanted to say. "Thanks."

117

Heidi nodded, pretending to be intent on adjusting a workbook in her bag, which she had remembered to snatch up off the lawn.

"You're welcome," she said without looking up. "I guess I've always admired you. You're getting so smart. Maybe you can teach me to play chess sometime."

Josh's eyes widened. He had always imagined Heidi — little Miss Superior — telling him how smart he was. Had his daydream come true? Or did he have a concussion from that hobnailed blow to the head?

Suddenly, they heard a yell.

"Mi-*chael*! Gladdy!" Mrs. Sturdevant called from the house. "Time to get ready for dinner! And bring that nice big boy!"

BE SURE TO READ THESE OTHER COLD, CLAMMY SHIVERS BOOKS.

THE HAUNTING HOUSE

WHEN CAITLIN MOVES INTO AN OLD HOUSE, SHE HAS A STRANGE FEELING SHE IS DISTURBING THE HOUSE'S PEACE. SHE IS BOTHERED BY STRANGE NOISES. WEIRD THINGS START TO HAPPEN. THINGS THAT CANNOT BE EXPLAINED. AT FIRST CAITLIN THINKS THE HOUSE MAY BE HAUNTED. BUT SHE SOON STARTS TO WONDER IF THERE IS SOMETHING AT WORK EVEN MORE FRIGHTENING THAN GHOSTS – AND MORE DANGEROUS. ALL SHE KNOWS FOR SURE IS THIS: SOME FRIGHTENING PRESENCE IN HER NEW HOME IS ALSO DEADLY.

LET, LET, LET THE MAILMAN GIVE YOU COLD, CLAMMY
SHIVERS! SHIVERS! SHIVERS!!!